Samantha's Portmanteau Tale

Derrick Garmonie Dogbe

ISBN: 0692673911

ISBN 13: 9780692673911

The Permission

It was a cool Friday evening in Abbotsville, a family-friendly community in New York. Children gathered together at the park to play like stars in the sky, but Samantha was in her room rehearsing with her keyboard as she had an upcoming concert with her school's orchestra.

Unable to believe the amazing sounds coming from the next room, her mom rushed over. "Wow! You are really good with the keyboard, Sami. And the song you were just playing always reminds me of your dad and how we met. Have I ever told you the story of how your dad and I started dating?" she asked.

"No, you haven't," replied Samantha.

"Okay, well, I think you are old enough to know now," she said with a smile. "On my twenty-first birthday, my friend took me to a party. It was fun. It's always fun getting to meet new people. While we were all hanging out, talking, and having fun, your dad, who was considered some guy back then, came into the party with his US Navy buddies. They had heard about the party and had decided to come and hang out for one more night before they boarded the ship.

"The owner of the house had a piano in the corner of the living room. I remember one of his friends said, 'Hey, Jake, play something for us, man!' He was reluctant. Then the rest of the guys chanted, 'Do it! Do it! Do it!' So he finally got up and sat at the piano. There were many other party songs that he could've played, but he chose to play 'You're the Inspiration.' It was a good song, so we all joined in and sang along. Your dad kept staring at me the whole time he was singing, and we kept eye contact until the song was over. He stirred up the party a bit. We clapped for him as he jokingly bowed down and said, 'Thank you, New York,' pretending to be a big star.

"For the rest of the night, your dad and I talked. I will admit that I didn't want him to leave. He was funny and amazing...and he still is. So I gave him my number and told him to call me whenever he got back. Two days later, I was in my room completing my assignment when I saw a strange number calling my phone. I didn't want to answer at first, but then I remembered I was awaiting a special call.

"When I picked up, he said, 'Hi, I'm calling for Kathy. Is she available?'

"'This is she,' I said.

"'Hey, Kathy, this is Jake from the party last week-end...the navy guy,' he said.

"So we started talking, and when he got back, the first person he found was me. This time he didn't have to leave for a while. It would be four months before he went back.

We were both always sad every time he had to report for duty, but we always kept in contact whenever he was away. Whenever his ship landed in a different country, he would always call me first.

"Your dad and I took a lot of trips. We would go and visit cities he didn't get to explore much because he'd spent most of his time on the ship whenever they landed in a different country. We spent one weekend in Paris, France. We had breakfast under the Eiffel Tower one morning. That morning at the hotel, I woke up, and your dad wasn't in the room. I got so scared because I thought he was kidnapped. I didn't know what to do. I wanted to call the police, but I thought that maybe he was just taking a walk outside. I was contemplating what to do, so I decided to wait for a little while, and if he didn't show up, I was going to call the French police. I sat on the bed and waited. A few moments later, he walked in with a box in his hand.

"'Where did you go? You scared me, Jake,' I said. 'I almost called the police.'

"He just smiled and said, 'I went to get breakfast for us. Put some clothes on. Let's go somewhere to eat.'

"So we went to the Eiffel Tower and sat in the grass by it and started eating. People kept staring, but we didn't even care. We just kept eating.

"Another time, we traveled to Spain, and we had a lot of fun there too. We rode a little canoe together over a lake. He picked a flower and put it in my hair."

"Is that the picture on the wall in the living room?" Samantha asked.

"Yes, it is," her mom replied. "When we were done with the canoe ride, it was getting dark, so he decided to take me to a sports bar and restaurant called Solo Para Ti, which means 'just for you' in Spanish. He and his buddies usually went there whenever they stopped in Spain. If you hit a bull's-eye in the darts game three times in a single day, this bar would put your favorite Spanish meal on their menu for a whole year. The bar was always crowded, but if your name was on the menu, you were served first. Your dad had won the game a few months prior to our trip, so his name was on the menu. He still had to pay for his food but at a discounted price. We ate the 'Jake's Tortilla Española,' and it was delicious. His meal came with the regular Tortilla Española but he added two pieces of rotisserie chicken, some broccoli, and a slice of key lime pie. The meal also included a drink of his choice, but the glass had his full name on it."

"I want to try that," said Samantha.

"Oh, this was years ago, Sami," her mom replied. "You weren't even born at that time. They don't have that anymore. Unless your dad played and won again, they had to take his name off the menu.

"One day he came back from Italy and asked me to marry him. I agreed without hesitation, and we got married. One year later, we had you, our little bundle of joy— our cute little angel who would always cry whenever we left the room. It seemed like you could feel or not feel my presence in the room. Sometimes I would close your room door and hide in the corner to pretend that I had left the room. You wouldn't cry even though you couldn't see me, but if I closed the door and stood on the other side, you would start screaming. It was like you could work magic!"

Samantha giggled.

"Samantha," her mom went on, "the reason I am telling you this story is because I want you to follow in my footsteps so you can have a great life. When you get older, you should only date a gentleman. It doesn't matter what racial or cultural background he's from. If he's a good person, someone who loves and respects you and is willing to take very good care of you, you guys will be great together."

"Hey, I have an idea, Mom," said Samantha.

"What is it?" asked her mother.

"Let's surprise Dad when he gets back."

"What do you mean?" her mother asked.

"As soon as we see the shuttle drop him off, we'll get ready. I will start playing 'You're the Inspiration' on the keyboard, and you start singing as soon as he walks through the door."

"Yes, let's do that. That will be great," said her mother.

"Would you like to practice now?" asked Samantha.

"Yes, let's practice. I don't really know all the words to the song, but I will learn it."

As they began to practice, suddenly the doorbell rang. "Are you expecting a visitor?" Samantha's mother asked.

"Yes, my friends Ava and Erica are supposed to come over so we can rehearse together, but they said they would be here at 6:30 p.m. It is only 5:45 p.m."

"Well, can you see who it is, please?" her mom asked.

"Sure, Mommy," she replied.

When Samantha opened the door, standing before her was her teacher.

"Hello, Mrs. Jones! Please come in."

"Hi, Samantha, how are you?"

"I am fine, thank you," Samantha replied with a smile. "How about yourself?"

"I'm well, thank you," Mrs. Jones replied. "Is your mom home? I would like to talk to her about what you and I discussed the other day."

"Yes, she is," replied Samantha. "Come in, and I'll get her for you."

"Thank you," replied Mrs. Jones.

Moments later, Mrs. Hanks came out.

"Hello, Mrs. Hanks. My name is Marina Jones, and I am Samantha's social studies teacher."

Samantha interrupted their meeting and said, "I will be in my room if you need me, Mom."

"Okay," her mom replied.

Then Samantha walked away.

"Hi, nice to meet you," said Mrs. Hanks to Mrs. Jones.

"You have a lovely home," replied Mrs. Jones.

"Thank you," Mrs. Hanks replied. "Please have a seat. So how can I help you?"

"I am here to talk to you about Samantha," Said Mrs. Jones.

"Uh oh! Has she been causing trouble?" asked Mrs. Hanks.

"No, she hasn't," replied Mrs. Jones. "Samantha is one of the best students in my class. She is always on time, and she sits in the front very quietly and attentively every period of my class. Moreover, she is very friendly and kind toward her classmates.

"But there's a saying that goes 'Good behavior and charity begin at home.' If you are very respectful and kind to your family at home, you will be respectful and kind to others. With that being said, I want to thank you for her upbringing. She is very generous too. I have seen her offer stationery to a fellow classmate who needed it."

"She really is a good kid," said Mrs. Hanks, "but it took a lot of time and effort to raise a well-rounded child like Sami. If you ask me, children are little rebels. They are rebellious against everything you say. For instance, a child would love to have ice cream or candy before dinner, but you know very well that it will ruin their appetite for whatever you are preparing for dinner. Also, too much sugar can sometimes cause hyperactivity—and you don't want that, especially right before bed. Someone with bad parenting skills would probably say no at first but would give in as soon as the kid started to cry. But a good parent will not relent. That was what I did and still am doing with Samantha. She wasn't born as this perfect child who listened to everything I say. She got angry a lot of times because I wouldn't let her have things that I knew were bad for her to have. Sometimes I felt bad for her, but deep down I knew what I was doing was good for her and that she would grow up to be a good child."

"Wow! I don't have any kids yet, but that is something to consider whenever I decide to have them. So thanks for the advice," said Mrs. Jones.

"As the coordinator of our new after-school programs, I am here today to ask you for permission for Samantha to be a speaker next weekend at the fright intervention program. This program is for little boys and girls who are frightened by imaginary creatures like monsters, ghosts, or just being in the dark. The program is sponsored by the board of education for all elementary schools, so the faculty approved one extracurricular hour after school to talk to these kids about their fears and how to get rid of them. As educators and members of institutions of learning, we realized that we have only been focusing on academics in schools. Our students are required to be good at studying, completing homework, and passing exams—basically, great at academics. But there are a lot more lessons to be taught. Parents drop off their kids to spend six hours or more at school, so we need to teach more than just academics.

"There are many things that occur outside of schools. Some kids struggle with self-esteem issues, and this is sometimes taken into adulthood. Others struggle with many types of bullying, including cyberbullying. We have come to the conclusion that we need to intervene and try to help them with these issues. So next week we are having the fright intervention program, and the week after that will be the bullying intervention and then the low-self-esteem intervention. But right now, we are focusing on fears.

"We have been contacting all the younger students' parents or guardians to inquire about their behavior at home. Sadly, we will have a hall full of candidates. Many children have this problem growing up. Children create a fear, and that's normal, but if it persists, that is when we step in. We have been working on many strategies for helping them, one of which is to bring in a speaker about their age or a little bit older to share his or her story with the students. We are hoping that they will relate more to that age group. There will be a little boy named Max who will be at the next intervention telling his story of how he conquered a very troublesome bully. Then the following week, we will have another speaker. This time it will be a girl named Sophia who will be talking to the kids about self-esteem.

"I introduced the program to my class today, looking for a possible candidate, and Samantha told me a story of how she was once scared of ghosts and monsters—and how you helped her get rid of those fears. I thought it was an interesting story, so after class I asked her if she would like to share her story with the students of our intervention program. She agreed but requested that I speak with you first."

"Well, that is great!" said Mrs. Hanks. "If she agreed to be a speaker, then I concur. The only thing I'm worried about is stage fright. I don't think she has spoken to a large group before. I remember her participating in a drama once, but her character was a tree, so she didn't get to say much. She is a little shy, but I think she can do it."

"I think so too, considering how well she participates in class," said Mrs. Jones. "She always answers questions, and sometimes she has to explain her work to the entire class. She usually does it pretty well. I forgot to mention that she will receive a gift from the school for telling her story. But it's a surprise, so don't tell her yet. Do you know what she likes?"

"I can't think of anything else besides a tablet she has been wanting," replied Mrs. Hanks. "It will be best to give her a gift card so she can make the purchase herself. She is very particular about the color and the specifications. Or maybe I can ask about it later in order to get more details."

"Okay, great. I will let the principal know," said Mrs. Jones..

"What you guys are doing is great—just great!" said Mrs. Hanks. "When I attended school as a young kid, there weren't any programs like that. Growing up, if you thought you weren't pretty enough, you always had that problem all through your life. There wasn't anybody to help you with that. Children are fast learners, especially at that age. They are aware of their surroundings. Sometimes the things they see in motion pictures and even still pictures can be processed in a negative or positive way, depending on the kid and the situation that he or she is in."

"That is true," replied Mrs. Jones. "Well, I am glad to talk to you today. Thank you for having me over. I am going to leave now. I don't want to use up all of your time, and I also have another family to meet with. Thank you very much."

"Yes, thank you for stopping by," Mrs. Hanks said to Mrs. Jones. Then she shouted to Samantha, "Sami, do you want to say good-bye to your teacher? She is leaving."

"Sure," she answered.

A few seconds later, Samantha came back to the living room.

"Good-bye, Mrs. Jones! I will see you on Monday," she said.

"Okay, bye-bye, Samantha. Don't forget to complete your assignment this weekend."

"Okay," Samantha replied.

"So, Sami, your teacher just asked me for permission so you can talk to the other kids. Will you be ready to tell your story to your schoolmates next Friday?" Samantha's mom asked.

"Yes, I think I can," Samantha replied.

"That is good, Sami. I will be there to see you."

The Speaker

A week later, the hall was filled with parents, students, and faculty. Mrs. Jones held the microphone and said, "Guys, as you find your seats, I would like you to know that there's a cooler full of drinks and a table of snacks in the corner to my right, so feel free to grab something before we start." Then she went to the back to talk to Samantha.

"Okay, are you ready, Samantha?" she asked.

"Yes, I am," replied Samantha.

"Is there anything you need before you start?" asked Mrs. Jones..

"Yes, I will need a chair to sit on because it might take me the whole hour to tell my story from start to finish."

Mrs. Jones grabbed a chair and set it on the stage. A few minutes later, everyone was seated.

"Hello everyone!" Mrs. Jones shouted.

"Hello, Mrs. Jones!" the crowd shouted back.

"I have a girl with a great story to tell you all today. Welcome, Samantha Hanks!"

The audience applauded as Samantha took the microphone.

"Hi guys. My name is Samantha, and I am here to talk to you all today. I know what you are thinking. 'How can a girl who is only a few years older than us convince us not to be scared?' Well, a few years ago, I was about your age, and I was afraid of everything—I mean anything and everything. But I am not afraid anymore. I can walk through a dark hall without fearing that a ghost or a monster will get me. You can be like me too. That is why I am here—to tell you how I got rid of all those fears. Here is my story. Not all of it is scary, and I might deviate from my topic, but it will all make sense at the end. So get ready, because it might get a *little* bit scary.

"Being scared as a kid is normal. In fact, people have had fears since the beginning of time. Whether you are trying to escape from a saber-toothed tiger or a mean bully, the fright is the same. Your heart beats faster, you make quick decisions, and you run faster than you normally would. Sometimes you can even jump higher than normal. However, my fear was not about tigers or bullies. *Phasmophobia*, or fear of ghosts, was what I struggled with. But this fear didn't appear until I was seven years old."

Samantha went on to tell the following story.

Samantha's Story Begins

One night in October, at 9:00 p.m., I turned on the television in my room—like I do some nights when I can't fall asleep—and a scary movie was on. Sometimes eating a certain kind of food or drinking a certain kind of drink before bed hinders my sleep. This was one of those nights. I don't remember what I ate or drank, but I couldn't fall asleep at all, so I decided to watch a little bit of TV. But nothing interesting was on the kids' channel, so I changed the channel to one of the grown-ups' channels, since there are over a hundred of those but only three channels for kids.

By that time, I had broken three rules that my mom had imposed, and she would not be happy if she found out. First, I violated my eight o'clock bedtime rule by staying up longer. Second, I turned on the TV after hours, and my mom said that watching TV after eight o'clock was prohibited. Third, switching to a grown-up channel was not allowed. So I would be in the biggest trouble if she found out.

After switching to so many channels, I finally found a movie. The movie might have started at nine o'clock because, when I switched the channel at 9:12 p.m., the name of the movie and the introductory credits were over. I thought it was a kids' movie because there was a boy in a field who seemed to be playing with a boomerang, and the next scene showed him getting very good at it.

"Oh great, a nice movie I can watch quietly until I fall asleep," I thought, considering that it was an hour past my curfew.

It seemed like a great movie at first, but then it started to get scary. What I did not know was that I had switched to a horror channel, and I would discover later that the movie I was watching was called *The Boomerang Ghost*. I had great hopes of just lying in bed and watching something interesting until I fell asleep, since I was all ready for sleep. My lights were off, the TV volume was low, and I was covered up with my Barbie blanket—except for my head.

But my hopes were shattered when the face of the boomerang ghost appeared on the screen. The scariest moment of my life was now in progress. Now I was sitting upright on my bed with my back against the headboard. My heart was beating really fast, and my mind was wondering if it was possible that this ghost could get me. I got even more scared as I imagined it.

I didn't really understand the movie when I watched it the first time because I was much younger back then, but I watched it again recently, so I was able to better understand it. It is about a Native American boy named

Cheveyo, which means "Spirit Warrior." In the movie, the city of Moenkopi had the most powerful weapon. It wasn't machine guns, chemical weapons, or robots. It was a person: a little boy.

Long ago, intruders used to come into Moenkopi to destroy the town, assault the occupants, steal their property, and sometimes do even worse things. This used to take place once or twice a year, until one day when Cheveyo was given the power to protect his city. At the beginning of the movie, Cheveyo was playing with his favorite toy, the boomerang. Every day, after he was done with his chores, Cheveyo would go into the woods to practice with his boomerang. Sometimes he wouldn't return until evening. He would be in the woods all day, chopping off fruit from the trees and trying to hit flying objects like birds. It seemed like it was always fun for him.

One evening while returning home, he fell into a pit, and he remained there for the next twenty-eight hours. His family went out looking for him but returned home without him. There was no sign of him anywhere.

Meanwhile, he was in the pit with a broken ankle and trying by every means possible to get out. There were some hanging vines that he thought he could hang onto, but they weren't strong enough, so he fell back in. Next, he tried stretching his legs, hoping he could move them from wall to wall until he got out, but one ankle was broken, so that was a bad idea also. He gave up and tried screaming once more, hoping someone would hear him and come to his rescue. But nobody could hear his scream. He was too far away from the town.

Then he heard an old lady say, "You are wasting your time, son."

She was wearing a long brown *mantas* and her hair was white and worn in a *chongo* style.

"Whoa!" he shouted. He'd had no idea he wasn't alone in the hole. "How did you get down here?" he asked.

"Oh, don't worry about that," she said. "What you should think about is how you are going to get out.

"What do you think I have been doing this whole time?" he asked.

"Well, I am your only hope, if you want to get out," she said.

"Yes, and I am *your* only hope, too," he replied. "So let's work as a team. You can stand on my shoulders, and when you get to the top, you can pull me out. How about that?"

"I meant I am your only hope because I can get out all by myself." Four seconds later, she levitated out of the hole. "See what I am talking about?" she shouted down from the top of the pit.

"Whoa! How did you do that? Are you a magician or something?" he asked.

"You can call me whatever you want," she said. "Now, in order for me to get you out of this pit, you have to promise me that you will protect this city if I give you the power to."

Cheveyo was hesitant at first, but he finally agreed. She told him that with his powers he could live forever—but only if he used them for a good cause. If he used his powers for evil, he would die.

"This city is counting on you, Cheveyo. Be a good kid now. I will see you later," she said.

"Wait! Where are you going? You can't leave me here. We made a bargain!" he shouted.

She looked back and said, "My work here is done. You have the power to do anything. All you have to do is just think it." Then she vanished.

"What does she mean by 'just think it'?" he asked himself. Then he thought, "I want out of this pit." One second later he disappeared and reappeared at the top of the pit. "No way. I have magical powers?" he asked himself.

He soon discovered that, with his powers, there was no limit to what he could do. But he had to be very careful how he used his powers, or they would be detrimental to his health, even if used accidentally.

He finally got home and was greeted by his worried family. They were glad he was alive. He told his family he fell in a pit where he'd been trapped for hours, but he had managed to get out. He left out the details of how he'd met a sorceress who gave him special powers. That would be a secret for a while but not for too long. He was eager to tell his father, who advised him to speak to the citizens of Moenkopi, since all of his powers were meant to protect them.

The people were excited after Cheveyo exhibited some of his powers. "The savior is here!" they said. "Farmland is cultivated in the blink of an eye, and the poor now live in better homes."

Now the city was blooming enough to attract more invaders. Weeks passed, then months, and one day the invaders got a break. This time there were hundreds of invaders, and they entered the city from every angle. They were burning down homes, stealing things, and destroying the city.

"Where is Cheveyo?" everyone cried out.

Cheveyo hadn't heard the bad news yet. He was at home and sleeping.

His dad woke him up. "Son, it is time! They are back again."

Cheveyo went out and saw that half of his city was on fire, and people were screaming for help. Moments later, Cheveyo duplicated himself. Now there were hundreds of him, and not too long after that, the intruders were conquered. There was only one alive, begging for his life. Cheveyo told the invader to leave the town, to never return, and to let the others know that the town was off-limits.

For the first time, Cheveyo had used his powers to protect his city. And many more years later, he would still be guarding his people. Everyone loved him. Cheveyo went to high school and met new friends. Many were jealous of him because he had the power to do anything he wanted. But some people were also afraid of him—for instance, the girl he liked.

Once, Cheveyo had asked Isabella to the prom, but she declined his request, so he grew angry. Just as Isabella and her friends were taking prom photos, Cheveyo ordered it to rain, and it rained heavily. The bad weather messed up Isabella's prom dress—and the occasion. That was the first time he had used his powers for evil, but there would be many other instances in which he would continue to misuse his powers. Remember, the sorceress told him that he could live forever only if he used his powers for good, but if he used his powers for evil, he would perish.

After many years of defending his city, Cheveyo died of an illness. The people mourned the death of their great guardian. Upon his burial, his mom asked that he be buried with his favorite toy, the boomerang. A couple of decades later, the city was developing into a modern city. Houses were being built everywhere, and new roads were constructed. The people of Moenkopi had completely forgotten about their great warrior, Cheveyo. Their museum, which included simple titles like "Who Caught the Biggest Fish," didn't include anything about Cheveyo. His burial site, which was supposed to be sacred land, was the birthplace of a new high school building. So Cheveyo's ghost grew angry and started killing the people of Moenkopi one by one. He claimed his first victim, the mayor of the city, at the opening of the high school.

What made the movie even scarier was that Cheveyo's ghost didn't cull a specific victim. Everybody was a target, and it didn't matter if it was a little kid or an adult. But he didn't strike when there were two or more people. He only harmed his victims when they were alone. The city was in total disarray. Police were on the verge of catching the serial killer. They figured out that he was smarter than them, and that was because the serial killer was a ghost. On TV, the news reporters asked citizens to stay calm, lock their doors, and avoid being alone if possible. Well, that made it even worse. The main reason no one knew this was being done by a supernatural being was because anyone who had seen it was dead.

All the police knew was that every victim was slain by a sharp object, so they decided to have a checkpoint where they searched every vehicle. Everyone with some sort of blade was a suspect. But the people were all carrying weapons in order to protect themselves from the serial killer on the loose. People realized that this only happened when someone was alone, so they started grouping up and keeping an eye on each other. But it was only so long before someone had to go and use the restroom or take a shower. And as soon as they shut the door or the shower curtain, they were gone. What a tormented way to live!

By this time, I wanted to change the channel, but I couldn't find the remote anywhere near me. This meant that I would have to get off my bed and walk up to the TV and push the power button. I didn't think it was a good idea to get off my bed, so I just sat there and watched the whole movie.

In the end, a little girl told her mom that she had a dream about a boy who was buried under the Moenkopi High School, and he was not happy. That was why so many people were dying. Her mom told the police.

After searching through the history of the city, they found the article about Cheveyo, the savior of the people of Moenkopi, who was buried in sacred ground. They excavated his body and reburied it in a tomb. They built a statue at the entrance to the city, and Cheveyo's story was put in the museum. Now Cheveyo had gotten what he wanted and what he deserved. The city was back to normal, and the people of Moenkopi were living their lives peacefully.

At the end of the movie, I quickly turned off the TV to avoid another scary movie. It was not unusual for me to watch a horror movie in October, but if I did, it was usually animated. And even if it was not a cartoon movie, at least at the end the beast would be slain, or the scary creature would turn out to be just someone pretending to be a scary creature. But this was no animated movie. It had real people, and it was very gory. And who's to say whether Cheveyo's ghost really did vanish? It seemed to me that he could come back at any time, and if he did, I didn't want him to attack me in my room. Then I decided I couldn't stay in my room. It was too quiet.

Sometimes I heard strange sounds in our house— even on normal nights. Our house was built in the early

1900s, and it's an old and very big wooden house that was restored. My parents admire older architecture, which is why they'd bought that house. They also like to entertain guests and members of our extended family, so there were many rooms in our house. There were five bedrooms on the same floor as mine. My room was farther down the hall, about fifty feet away from my parent's bedroom. The reason I picked that room was because it was the second room on that floor that had its own bathroom. I also played a lot of musical instruments, so I needed to be a little farther from my parents in order to avoid disturbing them. But this wasn't the best room to choose, especially in situations with ghosts! So I decided to take the risk.

Armed with a flashlight that contained some old batteries, I began an adventure. My goal was to spend the rest of the night lying beside my mom, hoping the boomerang ghost couldn't kidnap me from my mom's bed. But before I could achieve this goal, I had to go through a very dark hallway. I slowly opened my door and looked out. All I could see was complete darkness. I knew that, somewhere in the darkness, Mr. Cheveyo and a myriad of other scary creatures awaited me. As I walked through the valley of the shadow of death, I feared all evil. I couldn't see them, but I felt the presence of the scary creatures lurking in the darkness. The wooden floor made a crackling sound, and it echoed through the hall behind me, sounding like someone was following me. But every time

I looked back, there was nobody there—creature, ghost, or otherwise.

The bulb in the flashlight was flickering, due to low batteries. I thought if the batteries ran out completely, my situation would get worse, so I decided to run as fast as I could. I finally got to my mom's bedroom door. I couldn't rush into her room because I would be breaking another rule, which was to always knock on a closed door. With my back against the door while facing the hall, I banged on her door.

"Who is it?" she asked.

"It's me, Samantha. Can I sleep by you? I am very afraid to sleep in my room."

"Come in, sweetheart," she said. "Are you still afraid because of what Ricky said to you?"

"No, I'm just afraid to sleep in my room tonight, Mom. I had a bad dream," I replied. I couldn't state the main reason for my fear that night because it was possible that I would be punished for watching television outside of my curfew.

She asked about Ricky, my next-door neighbor, because he had said something very scary to me earlier that day. When I came home from school that day, I had seen Ricky on his front porch with his handheld gaming console. Ricky was four years older than me. Sometimes he acted like a big brother to me, and other times he was just mean. But I think that's how most older brothers are. My friends from school have older siblings, and whenever I go over for a visit, I notice they bother the younger siblings, not because they hate each other but because of the whole sibling-rivalry theory.

Ricky is a boy who says the most ridiculous things, and sometimes his stories seem so believable. Once, he told me that God was a photographer, and he takes pictures of us. Whenever it rains, lightning and thunder follow. Ricky says the lightning is a flash from God's camera, and the thunder is the clicking sound that a camera makes after the flash. God has the biggest camera, and that's why the clicking sound is so loud. And the rain is just God sweating profusely, considering he has to take so many pictures because there are more than seven billion humans on earth. He said the reason God takes these pictures of us is for him to create a yearbook so that, when we get to heaven, he can show it to us.

While sitting by Ricky and watching him play his game, I was eating an apple, and I accidentally swallowed a seed.

"Oops! I just swallowed a seed," I said.

He paused the game and said, "You do know what's going to happen next, right?"

"No, what do you mean?" I asked.

He said, "That seed will germinate, and it will start to grow in your stomach. By the weekend, it will turn into a big tree that will start to protrude through your body, causing you to die."

With my knowledge from science class, I knew plants needed soil, water, and sunlight to grow, so I said to him, "You're lying."

But he was very serious. Then he said, "Just think about it. Through your whole life, how many times have you eaten something that had a tiny bit of sand on it? Your body doesn't know how to get rid of sand, so it stores it in your stomach. And you drink a lot of water daily. So there you have it. You have everything that a seed needs to grow. Apple trees don't need a lot of sunlight. That's why they grow in the north and not the south. When the sun starts to shine again, as soon as you yawn or start to talk, a bit of sunlight will sneak its way into your stomach. The seed will germinate, and soon there will be branches passing through your ears, nostrils, mouth, and eye sockets. Then you will perish. You won't be able to attend school anymore because you will be dead. All your friends at school will be sad. There will be a candlelight vigil in memory of you, and there will be a funeral for you soon.

"I am really going to miss you a lot, Samantha," he said. "But when you get to heaven, I want you to do me a favor. Please tell God to send me all the new games, even the ones that will be coming out next year. I also want a new bike. Okay? Thank you." Then he patted me on the head and started laughing. What a meanie.

I went home and cried for a while. I was very sad and scared at the same time. I sat in a corner and waited for my mom, hoping she would come home soon so I could give her a hug and tell her I loved her before the seed started to grow.

When she came home and saw me sitting in the corner, she asked, "What's the matter, Sami?"

"I am going to die, Mommy," I replied, sobbing.

She dropped her purse and ran toward me and said, "Why, baby? What happened?"

When I told her what Ricky had said, she just laughed and laughed.

I thought, "I am slowly dying, and my mom is laughing at me! Why?"

Then she said, "He lied to you, Sami. Plants don't grow inside of human beings."

"That's what I said to him, but he was very persistent with his story."

Then my mother disproved his theory about seed growth by swallowing one right in front of me.

"See? You are not going to die," she said. "And if you do, I'm dying with you." She played with my hair. "Don't let Ricky fool you. Don't worry about anything. Go and get ready for dinner. I am going to have a talk with Ricky tomorrow."

I wasn't worried anymore, and I overcame that fear pretty quickly.

Meanwhile, I felt safe lying beside my mom. Then I remembered that if I fell asleep, I would be alone in my dreams, probably. And the main aim was never to be alone, because in the movie, Cheveyo attacked his victims whenever they were by themselves. In some scenes, the victims were not completely alone. There were people in the same house or building.

As soon as people shut their door, the next thing they would see was the partially decomposed body of the boomerang ghost. He had a boomerang that could increase in size, and once thrown by him it could chop off many of your body parts before it returned to him. He would walk toward you slowly while saying scary things. You might take a few steps back and try to run away as fast as you could, but he could just disappear from behind you and reappear in front of you again. Then you'd fall victim to the boomerang ghost.

I tried to stay awake the whole night. I just lay there with my eyes open, staring through the darkness. I tried not to even blink for a second, or I would get an instant vision of Mr. Cheveyo. I don't remember what happened the rest of the night, but eventually my mom's alarm clock started ringing.

"It's time to get ready for school, Sami. Wake up!" she said.

Then I realized I had been sleeping, but the boomerang ghost hadn't gotten me. "Maybe he was busy tormenting other people and forgot about me," I thought. "But I can never do it again. I can never fall asleep again," I warned myself.

Erica the Zombie Girl

The next morning, I saw Ricky at his bus stop, waiting for his school bus to pick him up.

I shouted, "Hey liar, I'm still alive!"

He replied, "I can't believe you fell for that. You are so gullible."

He was right. Why did I even believe anything he said, anyway? Sometimes when someone is older than you, it's easy to believe whatever he or she tells you, especially when you are just a little kid. In this case, Ricky had more seniority over me, so he could even convince me that the sky was maroon. Also, the manner in which he said things could make him seem trustworthy. You might say, "That's a lie, Ricky," because of your knowledge, but his facial expression would always convince you. He was always serious when he said things. And he always said, "It has happened before." That was exactly what he said when I asked him how he knew God kept a yearbook.

"The zombie girl told me when she came back from heaven," he answered. He was referring to my best friend, Erica, as "the zombie girl."

Before Erica and I became best friends, I knew her to be "the dead girl" or "the zombie girl." One day, Ricky and I were riding our bikes to the store. While riding past the blue-and-black house that is four blocks away from mine, he shouted, "Pedal faster! Pedal faster!"

I didn't know why, but I did what he said. Moments later, I asked why we had to go so fast.

"Did you see the girl sitting on the front porch all alone?" he asked.

"Yes," I replied.

"She is a zombie, and that's why she has no friends. Nobody wants to play with her, not even her closest friend. She died last year, and I attended her funeral. We were about to go through the burial process, but she came back to life. It was total chaos. Mourners were fleeing for their lives every which way. But I was the only one who was brave enough to talk to her. That was when she told me that God showed her the yearbook of everybody."

The story of Erica seemed true. Every time I rode past her house, she was sitting alone and seemed to be watching the kids playing at the playground across from her house. There was something odd about her. She always waved and said hi to me every time I rode by. I usually waved back, but I never stopped. In fact, I always increased my speed whenever I got to the house before hers. I once thought of stopping to meet her, but I was afraid. Sometimes she seemed like a normal girl to me. Her hair was always in a good style, and she was always dressed nicely. Most of all, she talked. Zombies cannot even say a word. They cannot smile and wave, either. They are always dirty, they walk crooked, and they are always in search of good flesh to eat. So if she really was a zombie, why wasn't she attacking the kids across from her? And why wasn't she chasing after me? Instead, she was sitting so politely and also sadly, and she was also nice and clean. So I decided to investigate the story about the dead girl.

One evening while at the dinner table, my mom and I were done eating, so I asked her about the zombie girl that lived four blocks away from us.

"That girl is not a zombie. She is perfectly fine," Mom said. My mom told me the real story, which Erica would later confirm. Erica was playing on the swing set one day, and she decided to do the eagle jump. The eagle jump is when you're riding the swing very high, and when it goes forward, you jump off in midair. Before landing, you scream, "I am an eagle!" and you land on your feet. I used to do that, and it was fun until I realized that I could get hurt very badly. That was exactly what happened to Erica. She was trying to do the eagle jump, but her sweater got stuck in the rope, so she was hitched by the swing, causing her to fall to the ground headfirst. Her dad called for the ambulance, which took her to the hospital, where she was pronounced dead. They tried to resuscitate her many times, but they failed every attempt.

Her body was sent to the morgue. It was a very sad story. It was all over the news. Mourners had a candlelight vigil in front of her house. The date was set for her funeral and everything else. Friends in the community came by to sympathize with her family. Then the strangest thing happened.

Back at the morgue, Erica's heart started beating again. She woke up and did not know where she was and how she got there. She was in a cold and dark drawer. She thought it was a prank at first. After a few minutes of shouting out for help and banging on the roof of the drawer, no one came to her rescue. So she successfully squeezed herself out. When she crawled out of the drawer, she noticed that she was in a big room with many tables. On the tables she saw what appeared to be some department store mannequins, but they were not. She couldn't figure out where she was and how she had gotten there.

She thought, "Who are these people, and why did they bring me here? Why don't I have any clothes on, and why are people on the table with cutting instruments by them? I need to find a way out without anyone noticing me. But first, I need to cover up." To her left, there was a rag, which she used as a wrap to cover her body. She hid under desks, behind doors, and against walls until she finally saw an exit sign. She also saw a man sitting at a desk. She decided to risk it and head for the doors.

As she ran out, the guy at the desk shouted, "Hey, little girl! Stop!"

But she didn't. She kept running as fast as she could. Luckily, there was a patrol car across the street. She ran to the cop screaming, "Help me!"

He stepped out of the vehicle and said, "Hey, kid, what is going on? Who's chasing after you?"

She told him where she was and how she'd managed to escape.

He took out his radio and said, "I have with me a missing girl, possibly a kidnapping victim. The victim claims there are many other victims where she escaped from. We are looking at a possible serial killer here. I mean, this guy could be dangerous, so send me some backup."

The responder asked for the victim's name.

"Erica Luel, age twelve. She's the daughter of Ed and Justine Luel."

"I can't believe it," said the responder.

"What do you mean?" the officer asked.

"I'm sorry, Lieutenant, but you are talking to a dead girl, sir. Her body has been at the morgue since Thursday."

The officer dropped the walkie-talkie and paused for a minute with his eyes wide open in disbelief.

"Um, did he just say I'm dead?" Erica asked.

"Yes, it must be a miracle," he said. "You have been considered dead for a day or two now, and the building you escaped from is a morgue. That's why there were other people on the tables. Oh my, how did this happen?" The officer picked up the radio from the ground and requested an ambulance.

"No, I don't want to go to the hospital again," said Erica. "I just want see my mom and dad!"

"Kid, we have to take you to the hospital to make sure you are well. Your parents are going to meet you there, okay?"

"Okay," she replied.

When the police called her parents, they couldn't believe what they were hearing, so they quickly ran to the hospital. There she was, lying in the hospital bed and healthy as a horse.

Friendship

Have you ever been to an animal exhibit and seen an animal you thought was adorable, but you were afraid to pet it because you thought it might bite off your fingers? But then later you were convinced that it was really friendly? It doesn't always have to be an animal. It could be a toy or anything. That was the similar situation with me and Erica. For the longest time, I knew Erica as the dead girl or the zombie girl. And what's the one rule to follow when you see a zombie? You run fast and stay away from it, or else you will make a good meal. That was my usual response whenever I saw her.

But not this day, especially now that I knew the true story and how she'd suffered. I didn't really have a best friend. I did have some friends at school, but I would have loved to be friends with someone who was close by so that when school is on a break, I would still get to play with her. I tried to figure out a way to get close to Erica.

"I wonder what she likes?" I asked myself. I could get her one of her favorite things, and maybe we could become friends. Then I remembered I once saw her painting pictures on her porch. I said to myself, "Maybe I should get her newer brushes and some paint. Painting is one of my favorite things to do, so we would probably have a lot of fun together. But where can I get some money to buy them?"

I asked my mom, "Mommy, can I get my allowance earlier than usual? I promise to complete all of my chores."

"But you don't get your allowance until the weekend," she said.

"I know," I replied, "but I really want to get something for Erica. I am hoping we can be friends."

"Oh, okay. That's great, Samantha. Here you go," she said. She handed me some money.

I went to the store to get some brushes and paint for Erica, but when I rode by her house, I noticed she wasn't sitting outside like she usually was. I still went to the store and got her the gift. When I came back to her house, she still wasn't outside, so I rang the doorbell. A few seconds later, a beautiful African-American lady came out. It was Erica's mother..

"Hi, how can I help you?" she asked.

"I'm here to see Erica," I responded.

"Listen to me," she said. "You kids need to leave my daughter alone. You guys walk by here and laugh at her to provoke her to anger, and I don't like that at all—not one bit! She was depressed for a while, and she is now in a good mental state, so please stay away from her. Please!"

I went home. I was sad because I really wanted to become friends with Erica. I grabbed a snack and started eating it. Then I decided to give it another try. I put the rest of the snack down on the table, grabbed the gift bag and my bike, and rode back to her house. I rang the doorbell. Her mom showed up again.

"Oh, it's you again," she said.

"Ma'am, I really want to talk to Erica, please. I am not here to bother her. I really want to be her friend. I got her something, and I want to give it to her."

"Oh, okay, hold on for a minute," she said.

Erica came out a few minutes later. I guess her mom told her someone wanted to befriend her.

"Hi, I'm Samantha," I said.

"Hi, I'm Erica," she replied.

"I got you something," I said. I handed her the bag.

"Thank you," she said as she took it from my hands.

"I saw you painting the other day, so I thought you might need more."

"I do need new brushes and some paint. Thank you for getting these things for me. I really appreciate it!"

"You're welcome," I replied.

"Do you want to come in? I can show you my paintings," she said.

"Yes, I do," I replied.

As I walked into her room, I realized that Erica and I had a lot in common. She loved to paint, and I did too. She loved to play music, and so did I.

As time went by, Erica and I became best friends—and we still are. We even do our chores together. We became leaf-raking buddies, which was always the fun chore. We would make a huge pile of leaves. Then, from a bench, we would jump into it together and wait for a few seconds and then jump back out with our arms spread out like a phoenix rising from the ashes. Sometimes we would throw the leaves up in the air, pretending they were confetti. That was fun too until we had to rake them all up again.

Once, we had to play detectives on the villain next door, Ricky. That day, Erica and I were done with her chores, so we came to my house to do mine. My chores for that weekend were vacuuming the living room and raking the leaves in the backyard. We decided to do the leaves first and then the living room. Usually we would bag the leaves and place the bags on the curb in front of the house for the garbage truck to take them. But this time we decided to pile them up, leave them there, clean the living room, and then come back and bag them later. We started cleaning the living room, and it was done in no time. It usually took me an hour or two to complete the vacuuming, but it took us twelve minutes. That is because I sometimes got distracted by something, and I would have to stop working for a while. Teamwork always got the job done faster. I was glad to have Erica on my team.

After we were done cleaning the living room, Erica decided we should take a break before going back out into the backyard—and our break should include a challenging game of *Just Dance*, the video game.

"Are you ready to take back the championship from me in *Just Dance*?" she asked.

"Bring it on," I replied.

We played for a while, but I couldn't win the championship. She was too good at that game. But it was a ton of fun. We needed to have some fun because we had been working all day. Anyway, we went back out to bag the leaves, and then we realized someone had scattered the big pile of leaves we'd made. We were devastated. We had to pile them all up once again.

"I wonder who would do this," said Erica.

"I thought it was my dog, Ajax, but he was inside with us the whole time," I replied.

"I bet it was your neighbor," she said.

"Probably," I responded. "You know what? We should try to catch him in the act!"

"Yeah," she said. "Let's pile them up again and go inside and watch from the windows."

So we did, and sure enough, here came Mr. Ricky. He looked around to see if anybody was watching. We crouched under the window, and then, a few seconds later, we looked out again, and he was kicking the leaves everywhere. So we went through the front door and around the house.

"Gotcha!" Erica shouted.

He was startled, and he started to run toward his house.

"Where do you think you're going, mister?" I asked. "You need to rake the leaves, bag them all, and put them on the curb."

"Or what?" Ricky asked.

"Or else I will tell your mom what you did when she comes home," I replied.

That said, he quickly grabbed the rake and started making piles of leaves and bagging them too. We just sat there and watched him complete our task. A few minutes later, all the leaves were in the bags.

"Okay, I'm done," he said.

"No, you're not," I said. "You need to take them all to the curb."

"I'm not going to do that," he said.

"Remember, I can still tell your mom," I said.

He didn't say anything that time. He begrudgingly grabbed the bags and took them to the curb. Erica and I just high-fived each other and laughed. The best weapon to use against Ricky is the statement, "I will tell your mom." His mom punishes him every time he does something wrong, and her punishments are usually extreme. That's why he's afraid to do wrong whenever she is around. Sometimes she seizes his video games for up to three months, and sometimes he is grounded for a whole month or longer. I was never going to tell his mom. I was just using that to scare him—and it worked. I didn't want to be the reason he was grounded. Sometimes when he was not allowed to come out for a month, I missed him, even though he troubled me a lot. But in order for me to be a hero or heroine, there had to be a villain. Without one, I was just a normal person.

Erica was such a great friend, and she was my third-favorite person in the world. She said a few months ago that she was very depressed, and she used to sit at home all day by herself. Everybody ran away from her. Nobody wanted to play with her because she was the girl who died and came back to life, or to say it simply, the zombie girl. I used to run from her too, but that was because I really didn't know the true story. If you really wanted to know what was going on around you, you wouldn't ask Ricky. If he were a news reporter, people would always get the wrong story.

Erica was friends with a girl named Ava before the accident. She thought Ava was a good friend, but she wasn't. Since Erica had left the hospital, Ava had never stopped by her house to visit her and wish her a speedy recovery. Even after one year, she still hadn't said anything to Erica. In fact, it was Ava who started the rumor that Erica was a zombie. What a meanie, right? She was so unkind.

Well, Erica is very happy with how things are going with her life right now. She said she is glad to have me as a friend, and I am glad to be friends with her too. She is no longer taking medications for depression anymore, because there haven't been any mean kids calling her names lately. That is because we hang out a lot, so they can see that she is just normal.

Erica and I are in the same grade this year. She is a year older than me, but she had to quit school for a year because she had to undergo many medical tests after the swing accident. I am glad we take the same classes together. Sometimes we study together whenever we have an exam coming up, and we usually quiz each other. This way, the exam is not a surprise, and we usually pass with flying colors.

Last Christmas, Erica and I raised some money because we needed it for a special occasion. Our class was challenged by Mrs. Jones, our social studies teacher, to do something nice for someone who needed it—an act of kindness for a less fortunate person or group of people. As an assignment, we had to write about it, explaining why we chose to help, how we helped, how the receiver felt, and how we felt. We also had to write about any obstacles that almost prevented us from helping, whether funny or not.

There was a homeless man and his dog always sitting at the stop sign by Erica's house. He usually held a sign that said, "Disabled veteran. Please help. Anything will do." Erica suggested that goodwill should include him and his dog, so we decided to bake cookies for donations. With the help of my mom, we were able to bake some delicious cookies. We set up a cookie stand at the intersection by my house, with a sign that said, "For charity. Please help."

Within an hour, our stand was crowded. My mom had to keep baking more cookies because we were running out too fast. I noticed it wasn't only about the taste of the cookies, but people also wanted to help. Some people paid

$20 for a cookie, and a man paid $112 for three cookies. It was not too surprising that people loved to give during the Christmas season. By the evening time, the crowd was reducing, and it was getting late, so we decided to close down the cookie stand. We made a lot of money that day.

The next day, we set out to buy some things for the homeless guy. We had enough money that we were able to buy a lot of things, including a jacket, a pair of boots, some blankets, some toiletries, and food for his dog. There was still a lot of money left. We didn't know what else to buy with it, so we put it in a box and wrapped it as a Christmas gift.

My mom took us to see the homeless guy, and we gave him the things we had bought for him, and we told him how we earned the money. He cried, and then we cried too. His name was Private David Valinsky. He used to fight for our country. As we were leaving, I looked back and saw him admiring the jacket we got him. I could tell he was very appreciative.

It felt good to help someone in need. I loved to see the smile on people's faces whenever they received something they really needed. He could now enjoy some things for a few months, things that I enjoyed every day without even noticing. The main idea for the assignment wasn't for us to gain points but to get in the habit of helping people in need.

I wish I could have helped that poor guy every week, although I hadn't seen him at that intersection since we donated the things to him. I always wondered where he was. Then my mom said he might be at another intersection asking for some more stuff. Well, I don't blame him because all he got was just a few things. Every time I was riding through an intersection, I always hoped to see him and his dog. I usually had some change with me just in case I saw him again. But I never did.

Weeks went by, and then months. One day I came home from school, and the moment I walked through the door, my mom said, "Sami, come to the living room."

When I got there, she showed me a picture. "Do you remember this guy?" she asked.

"No," I responded. "Why do you ask, Mom? Do you know who he is?"

"Yes, I do, and you know him too. Remember the homeless guy that you and Erica helped last December?" she asked.

"Yes," I replied.

"This is him."

"There's no way that is him. Oh, is this the 'before' picture?" I asked.

"What do you mean?" she asked.

"I mean the picture he took before he became homeless," I replied.

"No, this picture is recent. The guy's name is Dave, and he is not homeless anymore. He was on TV talking about his life and how it has been transformed all because of two little girls. And he wants to thank them in person.

So I called Erica's mom, and I also called the number to the local channel, and there will be a journalist coming to interview you guys. Dave will be here too."

"Wow! I'm going to be on TV. That's awesome," I said.

♦   ♦   ♦

It was Saturday, and Erica and I were playing *Just Dance* while my mom was giving Erica's mom a tour of our house. Soon there was a knock on our door. When my mom opened the door, Dave and the news crew were standing outside of our house.

"Hello, we are from LCTV. Are you Mrs. Hanks?" the news lady asked.

"Yes. Come in, guys," said my mom.

The interview went well. Dave was still very thankful for our kindness toward him. As he was talking about the huge impact we had made on his life, I realized that he and my dad had something in common. They both fought for our country, and they had a beautiful little girl that they cared a lot for. The only difference was that Dave's daughter, Blair, was no longer alive.

"It all happened in the blink of an eye," he said. "One day I had two amazing people that I loved and cared about, and the next day, they were both gone in an instant. I was on deployment in the Middle East when my commander told me that my family was in a fatal accident. They were killed by a driver who was texting and driving.

I was in shock and couldn't comprehend it. Even to this day, I still can't believe they're gone.

"Just a few days before the accident, I got a package from home. In the letter, my daughter wrote that she loved me and missed me a lot. And she included a picture of herself wearing a gold medal she had won for swimming. This was the second gold medal she won, and I missed both competitions. I lost the two people I loved—while trying to protect them. I love my country, but family comes first. Since I didn't have anybody to care for and nobody to care for me, I didn't reenlist for the military. I was depressed for more than a year. The bank foreclosed on my house because I couldn't afford my mortgage anymore. That's why I was on the streets begging for money, mostly to buy alcohol because I had nothing to live for.

"Then, last December, I met these two little angels who made me rethink my life and get off the streets. These girls stopped by and gave me a lot of things, including some new clothes, which I wore to my job interview. I am now the managing director of Tidy Up Car Care, and my life is back on track. It's not totally a normal life anymore, but I am doing a lot better than I was the past few years.

"So I am here today to thank you girls. I am very grateful for what you did for me. You girls remind me of my daughter, Blair. She was a great kid, and she always tried to help other people. All I have left of Blair are these gold medals, her dog, and some pictures. So I want you guys to have her medals. Just remember, every time you hold these medals, there's a little angel smiling down at you from heaven." With tears in his eyes, Dave handed us the medals.

"Thank you," we said to him.

It is very sad whenever someone dies, but it is even sadder when the person is a kid. I wish Blair hadn't had to die. I would have loved to meet her. We could have been friends. She sounded like an awesome person.

The next day, the story was on the news, and when we got to school, everybody was clapping for us. We felt like celebrities for a while. I loved being friends with Erica. We also signed up for the school orchestra, and it was amazing. I could play almost every instrument, and Erica was getting super with the instruments too.

We were having so much fun the other kids were starting to come around. Erica wasn't the dead girl or the zombie girl anymore. She was now called "the miracle girl." Of course, she did not like any of those names, so she would just say, "My name is Erica."

Friendship Two

There's another friendship I haven't mentioned yet. It is with another amazing girl, Ava. Earlier, I told you guys about a mean girl named Ava who used to be friends with Erica. It turns out Ava was not really mean. She was just abiding by what her mom told her about her best friend. When Erica had the accident, Ava's mom told her to wait just a little while before she could play with Erica. While Erica was undergoing some tests and treatment, people from the community thought she might be mentally disabled, and she might harm her friends accidentally. The rumor that Erica was a zombie girl derived from the fact that the other students from the class realized that even Erica's best friend wouldn't hang out with her, so they started it and blamed it on Ava.

Our friendship with Ava was the result of persuasiveness from me and forgiveness from Erica. I don't blame Erica for all her anger toward Ava. If I were in her shoes, I would be angry if my best friend did that to me.

One weekend, Erica and I were playing a game of *Guitar Hero*, and it was time well spent. After the game was over, we sat in my room and talked for a while. The main focus of our discussion was forgiveness. One of the greatest lessons my mom ever taught me is about the willingness to forgive. It is always hard to forgive someone who has hurt you, but if you do, that feeling is much better than the feeling of resentment and anger you had toward that person. I'm not sure Ava and Erica ever would have mended their broken friendship if I hadn't told Erica about forgiveness.

It was Ava's birthday weekend, and everybody was talking about the awesome party her parents were planning. Then, on Thursday evening, Ava contracted chicken pox. The party was canceled because nobody wanted to attend a sick girl's birthday party, regardless of how delicious her cake was. It was a sad day for Ava. She just sat in her room and cried all day.

While I was at home reading, Erica came over. "Guess what, Sam?" she asked.

"What?" I replied.

"Tomorrow is Ava's birthday, but she is sick with chicken pox," she said with a laugh. "All her friends are staying away from her, like she did to me. Let her see what it feels like. Maybe I should start a rumor that she is turning into a crocodile."

We laughed.

"That would be hilarious, but don't do it," I said.

"Why not? Kids will believe anything you say to them," she said.

"I know, but we should not fight evil with evil," I replied. "It would be a lot of fun to see kids calling her names, but there's a difference between us and Ava. The reason we are best friends is because we are two good people. If we do to her what she did to you, that means we are no different from her. To prove to her that we have good hearts, let's go and visit her tomorrow."

"I don't want to visit her. Why would I? We weren't even invited to her party in the first place," she said.

"You need to forgive her, Erica," I said. "Maybe we can all be friends. Instead of 'the two besties,' we can be 'the three amigas.'"

She chuckled and said, "Okay." Then she asked, "Have you had chicken pox before?"

"No," I replied.

"Well, I have, and you can only contract the virus once per lifetime. It is very contagious, so you will need to wear a protective suit, because you will contract the virus if you go in there."

"If you have had it before, and you are still alive, I think I will risk it," I said.

"Are you sure?" she asked.

"Yes, I will be fine. My main aim is to see you guys become friends once again," I replied.

The next day, Erica and I set out to Ava's house after the bus dropped us at our stop.

"Hey, Erica, I thought it would be better if we got two cards for Ava—one for her birthday and the other for her illness. Both of us can fill out her cards, but in the get-well card, you can wish her a speedy recovery and also write about your forgiveness. Let her know how you felt when you were ill and nobody came to visit you, and tell her you are not going to treat her the same way. We should also get a can of soup. I always want to eat soup whenever I'm ill."

"I can do that, but I will have to say it to her because I don't have any money right now to get her a card or two," she said.

"I have seven dollars," I replied.

"I think that is enough to get two cards and a can of soup," she said.

When we got to Ava's house, her dad was in the garage working on his car.

"Hello, Mr. Komatsu," said Erica.

"*Konnichiwa* girls," he responded in Japanese while bowing.

I don't know what *konnichiwa* means in Japanese, but I think he meant, "Hello girls."

"The party was canceled because Ava is very sick," he said.

"We know. We just want to wish her a happy birthday and a speedy recovery. Is she home?"

"Yes, she is in her room," he said.

We found Ava in her room, watching TV.

"Hi, Ava," I said. "How are you doing?"

"Hey, guys, I'm not well. I have chicken pox, and you don't want to touch me or else you will get sick too," she said.

"Oh, I'm fine," said Erica. "I've had chicken pox before, but Samantha hasn't."

"You shouldn't come too close, Sam," said Erica.

"Okay," I replied.

"We got you something," said Erica. "It is a birthday card, a get-well card, and a can of soup. We thought we should come and visit you, since nobody else showed up, even though we didn't get an invitation. Actually, it was Samantha's idea for us to come here today. I was still mad at you for not being there for me when I needed you. You also started a rumor that I was a zombie girl, and you stayed away from me since then. I am not mad anymore, because I have forgiven you for everything. Samantha talked me into forgiveness."

"I am so sorry, Erica," said Ava. "My mom was just afraid that you might have changed after your accident, so she said that I needed to stay away from you for a little while. There are not a lot of people who died and came back to life. That's why my mom was afraid of you. But I wasn't. I was just following my mother's rules. I was always hoping and praying that you would get better. I used to draw pictures of you and me hanging out. See?" Ava leaned over and grabbed her scrapbook and flipped to the first page.

"This is us playing hide-and-seek in the park like we used to do," Ava said. "And there are many more pictures of us in this book. And as for the rumor, I didn't start it. It was Jared Jenkins, or J. J. You know the kind of kid J. J.

is. You can ask everyone in my class. Last year he asked me why I wasn't hanging out with you. He didn't even give me a chance to answer. Then he said, 'Is it because she's a zombie now?' And that's how everybody started calling you the zombie girl. I missed you, Erica."

"I missed you too," said Erica. And they hugged.

"I am so sad because today is my birthday, and I'm in bed all day," said Ava.

"I have an idea," I said.

"What is it?" they asked.

"Let's ask your dad to buy us some body paint. We can cover you up so that your chicken pox is not noticeable. Then maybe we can go to the amusement park or the movies or somewhere. That way, we can take you to fun places for your birthday. And we can paint ourselves too so you won't look weird with us."

"You guys would do that?"

"Oh, that would be fun. Let's do it," said Erica.

"Okay, great. Let's go and ask my dad," Ava said.

So we went to find her dad. He was still in the garage working on his car.

"Hey, Dad, can you do us a huge favor, please?" Ava asked.

"Sure, anything for you, kiddo," he said.

"I feel a little better now and my friends want to take me places for my birthday, but there's a rash all over me. So they want to cover the rash with some body paint. They are also going to paint themselves."

"That sounds like fun," he said. "I assume you guys will stay far away from other people, right?" Because you don't want people to get sick because of you.

"Yes, we will," Ava replied.

"In fact, I want you to take some antibacterial wipes with you so you can wipe down everything you touch. Also, don't forget to cough and sneeze in you handkerchief only—not in the air."

"Okay Daddy," Ava replied.

"Great, I will run to the store quick and get some body paint. Is there a certain color you guys want?"

"Yes, let's do our favorite colors. Mine is purple," said Ava.

"Mine is blue," I said.

"Mine is red," said Erica.

"Well, Ava, you might want to do a darker shade of purple because it will cover up your skin better," he said.

"Better yet," I said, "we can all do a darker shade of our favorite colors and have all three colors painted on us to show we are united."

"We should do that," said Erica.

"Okay, great. I will be back, girls," he said.

"Okay," we responded.

"So where do you want to go, Ava?" I asked.

"I'm not too sure yet," she replied. "I need to ask my dad for some money. And where we can go depends on how much he gives me. I hope he gives me enough money. He was going to spend a lot of money on my party anyway. Now I know that the party doesn't matter because the two important people are right here to spend my birthday with me."

When Ava's dad got back, he gave her $150, which was more than enough money for us to have fun. First we went and got ice cream, and then we went to see a movie. We couldn't decide between two good movies, so we saw both of them. Next, we went to Ton o' Fun, the amusement park. Our experience was just what the place is called: a ton of fun. We felt like the three musketeers. People kept staring at us, but we didn't care much because we knew that was going to happen. We were there for the fun.

That day was one of the best days I have ever had, not only because of the fun part of the day but also because I helped mend a broken friendship. Prior to that day, I had thought Ava was a bad person. It turns out she is incredible, and I am glad we are all friends now. Every day is amazing when I have my friends around.

But sure enough, two days later I had chicken pox. I knew I was going to contract it sooner or later, considering that it was spreading throughout the school. I'm just glad I contracted the virus while in the process of doing something good. Besides the itching and a slightly elevated body temperature, my illness wasn't too bad, especially since I had my two friends by my side the whole time. That's what friends are for.

My friends and I do everything together—from making decisions about what game to play to making money to spend on a special occasion. And I like that my friends are from a different racial and cultural background. We celebrate everything together. Sometimes they come over to my house for Thanksgiving dinner, and it is always fun. And we get to celebrate New Year's Day twice every year. Ava's family is awesome. They are from Asia, and their New Year's Day falls on a different day than ours. And Erica's parents teach us more things about Black History each year, and I learn a lot every year.

About three weekends ago, we were able to raise some money again like we did last December. But this time it was for a different purpose. I was watching TV a few weeks ago, and I saw a commercial about the *Princess Lucinda Musical*. It was coming to theaters soon. "I have to see this," I said to myself.

On our way home from school the next day, I told my friends about the musical.

"Guys, guess which musical is coming to theaters soon?" I asked.

"Hmm, I can't think of anything," said Erica.

"It's the musical to our favorite movie," I said.

"*Princess Lucinda*," said Erica.

"Yes, it will be in theaters about a month from now," I said.

"Oh, we have to see it," said Ava.

"We should," I responded. "It is a bit expensive, though."

"So we need to ask our parents for some money," said Erica.

"It's a lot more than our allowances," I responded.

For a few minutes, we tried to figure out how we could make some money for the musical.

"I know how we can make some money," said Ava.

"How?" we asked her.

"Let's do what you guys did last December when you raised money to help the homeless guy and his dog. But this time, instead of a cookie stand, we can do a lemonade stand because it is summer."

"Yeah, that is a good idea," said Erica.

"Since the play won't be in theaters until a month from now, we have three weekends to raise enough money to buy the tickets. Let's ask my mom to be our coordinator again," I said.

"Okay," they replied.

My mom is awesome. She likes to participate in everything I'm doing. I knew that, with her help, we would do great with our lemonade sales. When we got to my house, my mom was in the laundry room doing some laundry. So we went in and asked her.

"Sure," she replied with a smile. "So do you guys' parents know about the play yet, Ava and Erica?"

"No, not yet. But we will ask for their permission today," Erica answered for both of them.

"Okay," my mom said. "Girls, since we've got three weeks until the play, we can do different flavors each weekend. What do you guys think?"

"Yes, that sounds good," Ava responded.

"We could do raspberry lemonade for the first weekend, strawberry for the second, and fresh peach lemonade for the last weekend."

"That will be awesome. Let's do that," I said.

For the next three weekends, we sold lemonade and made a lot of money. Accompanied by my mom, we were able to go to the musical, and it was awesome.

The Deception

I know by now you guys are sick and tired of hearing about Ricky. I am too. Who does he think he is? He is sort of a bully but probably not a bad one. At least not the kind that takes your lunch money, beats you up in the alley, and gives you a wedgie. Even though I am a lot older now than I was back then, he still tries to convince me about some of his lies, and he also still tries to pull pranks on me. He tried the milk-color theory but that was quickly eliminated because I knew what the truth is. He said white milk comes from white cows, and chocolate milk comes from brown cows. Somebody said that to me before, but I didn't fall for it then, either. His pranks don't work anymore. I am older and wiser now. Or at least I thought I was.

Just a few days ago, I was playing hopscotch in my backyard with my friend Erica.

Then I heard Ricky screaming, "Help me, Samantha! I'm bleeding."

So we stopped the game and ran to his house. When we got there, I saw so much blood on his hands.

"What happened?" I asked.

"I was trying to open a can of beets, and it sliced my palm open," he said.

I was worried he was going to pass out because he was losing so much blood.

"Let's call 911," Erica suggested.

"No, don't call them!" Ricky shouted.

"My mom said it is always best to call 911 whenever something like this happens," Erica said.

While they were deciding whether or not to call for help, I ran and grabbed the first-aid kit from their bathroom. I was scared for him but also excited because I'd get to do my first nursing job.

As I got closer to the wound, he said, "Just kidding! It's beet juice Ha-ha! Gotcha!"

"Oh, come on, Ricky!" I shouted. "One day you will really need my help with something serious, and I'm not going to help you."

"Yes, that was not cool, Ricky," said Erica.

"Come on Erica, let's go back to our game," I said. I was very upset, but he didn't even care. He just kept laughing as we left angrily. But just thinking about it now, it is a little hilarious. He's a good prankster. No wonder his name means "ruler" in the Indian language. He is the king of pranks.

I used to wonder why Ricky was the way he was. Then one winter break, his big brother, Raj, returned home from college. I noticed how much they loved each other, but I also noticed how they tormented each other. One day Raj poked holes in some soy-sauce packets and put them in the pockets of Ricky's khaki pants. Ricky was so angry at his brother after he sat on a bench and the sauce ruined his pants. So, in revenge, Ricky cracked some eggs and put them in Raj's new pair of shoes he'd gotten for Christmas.

Raj said, "I will get you back. You will not see it coming." Then he put cayenne pepper in all of Ricky's socks, and Ricky's feet were burning all day. He failed every attempt to prank his brother. Then winter break was over, and Raj went back to college. They were a bit mean to each other, and sometimes it was fun to watch, especially seeing Ricky being tormented for a change.

Ricky used to bother me a lot, but he would always fight to protect me whenever I was being attacked by another kid or bunch of kids—just what a typical big brother would do. Ricky's mom, the lady who makes the most delicious Indian cuisine, and my mom are best friends. Sometimes he had to watch me when they went out. One day he took me to the store to get my favorite game. While waiting in line, a boy jumped the line ahead of me and took my spot. Ricky got very angry and pulled the boy out of the line in order for me to acquire my original spot. Another time—this was my birthday—he gave me his new train set as a birthday gift. So he wasn't mean all the time.

Reading *The Ghost in the Backyard*

It had been two weeks since I watched *The Boomerang Ghost*, but it still seemed like the night before. My fears kept getting worse. I was fine during the daytime, but when it started to get dark, my fear came back. The darkness was now one of my greatest enemies, and sleep was the other one. I had a huge problem with anyone who told me to take an afternoon nap, because the last thing I wanted to do was close my eyes—not even to mention sleep.

Even the thought of being in a room alone was frightening. I started disliking brushing my teeth and taking a shower because both required washing my face, which also required me to close my eyes. So I came up with a system that would help me stay vigilant. I started washing one side of my face at a time. That way I could keep at least one eye open in case Mr. Cheveyo showed up in my bathroom. Then maybe I would be able to see him in time to yell for help.

I thought, "If only this was possible at bedtime, but it's not. You could never sleep with one eye open." It would have been great to switch eyes every four hours of sleep.

That would mean I could be half-asleep and half-awake for eight hours. But I had to keep in mind that the main idea was never to fall asleep, whatever I did. I was probably the youngest person with insomnia.

"How do I get rid of my insomnia?" I asked myself. First of all, I could never tell my mom the reason I hadn't been sleeping well, because I could possibly get a punishment. I would have to tell her that I turned on the TV after eight o'clock on a school night, which was a flagrant violation of her rules. After I had asked to sleep beside her for many nights, my mom finally asked me to tell her the reason I had been afraid every night, or else I would have to sleep in my room that night. I finally told her about the movie, but first I made her pinky-promise that she wasn't going to punish me. She agreed. Over the next few days, she tried to figure out a way to help me.

My mom had told me once that reading makes you knowledgeable, and it might make you smart, so she made me read two books each week that weren't related to school. To some kids, it might have seemed like a punishment, but I loved to read, so it was not a problem. She stopped by the library or bookstore every week to get books for me. They were always interesting to read, except for one that didn't seem like it would be interesting at all. It was called *The Ghost in the Backyard*. I hadn't read the book yet, but based on the title, I knew it wouldn't be my favorite.

That Thursday evening, my mom said, "Sami, you have to read this book after school tomorrow, okay?"

"Okay," I replied. Even though I was told to read the book, I didn't. What I read was the synopsis, in case she asked me to explain the story to her. I could just make up a scary story about a ghost.

It was 5:45 p.m., and my mom had just gotten home from work. Eager to know how I felt about the story, she asked, "So what did you think about the book, Sami?"

I just smiled and said it was a wonderful story.

She asked, "Can you tell it to me?"

"Sure, I replied. "There was a scary ghost in the town, and everybody was afraid, so they called the ghost hunter, but he was busy at his other job. So everybody decided to skip town until the ghost hunter left work and got his ghost hunting instruments to hunt the ghost—"

Before I could finish the first paragraph of my completely made-up story, she said, "Let me stop you right there. You did not read the story. You lied to me, and I am so angry at you right now. I read the book. That's why I brought it home for you. Now go to your room, and do not come out unless you have read the entire book."

From that moment on, I thought that was the greatest punishment ever imposed on me by my mom. I had to sit in my bedroom all by myself and read a book called *The Ghost in the Backyard*. I cried and cried for a while, because I was too afraid of being in my room by myself.

Then I realized crying would not solve my problem, so I decided to take the risk and read it.

The story was about a boy named Mateo. He was seven, the same age I was at the time. One stormy night, part of the tallest tree in the backyard broke off its trunk and hit his window. He was awakened by the loud noise. He couldn't fall back to sleep, so he decided to see about the damage to his window. When he looked out the window, what he thought he saw was an army of monsters coming to attack him from his window. So he quickly shut the window and got under his bed to hide himself from the savage creatures. He stayed under his bed for a while, hoping that when the monsters came to his room they would realize he was not there.

After a few minutes, he decided to check again, and the monsters were still in the same spot. He thought they must be stuck in the mud, or maybe they were really slow. Just as he went to shut the window again, lighting struck, and he realized that they were the same little palm trees that had been growing in the backyard all along. So he felt relieved. He decided to enjoy the cool breeze at the window until he got sleepy again. He stood there with his arms resting on the window sill, looking into the backyard. Beyond the trees was a white figure, and it seemed to be moving in a uniform motion.

"Ghost! Ghost!" he shouted.

While reading this part, I noticed that Mateo must have been thinking that ghosts were more powerful than monsters, because he could find his way around monsters, but with a ghost he needed help.

A few minutes later, Mateo's dad came running into his room. "Mateo, are you okay? And why is your window open?"

"No. I saw a ghost," he replied.

"Where?" his dad asked.

"Just look in the backyard. It's coming to get me!" he cried.

His dad looked out the window and saw the same white figure. "Oh! You're right. Come with me." His dad quickly took him downstairs and hid him in a little closet and said, "Stay here, okay?"

"Okay," Mateo replied warily.

His dad went out through the back door with a lantern and a kitchen knife to investigate the ghostly figure.

As I was reading that part, I thought, "Why is he going to attack a ghost with a kitchen knife?" I thought ghosts were supposed to be a hologram of a person. It's not impossible to stab a ghost, but it just didn't make any sense to do that, because they could pass through closed doors—if they were real.

Meanwhile, Mateo sat very quietly in the closet, awaiting his dad's return. He kept his hands over his mouth in order to avoid making any noise. He was very still and did not move at all. All of a sudden, he heard a squeaking sound as the door opened slowly. Then someone was standing at the door. Lightning flashed, and he could only see a silhouette of the person standing there. He shut his eyes and tried not to scream.

Then his dad said, "It's okay, Mateo. It's me. You can come out now. It wasn't a ghost in the backyard. It was just your mom's white nightgown she hung up to dry, and she forgot to bring it in." Then they both laughed and hugged, and they said good-night and went back to bed.

I realized the story was not scary at all. It was just the title of the book. There's a saying that goes, "Do not judge a book by its cover." That is true. I thought for sure there would be a scary ghost in the story. That's why I didn't want to read it at first. I felt a little relieved after reading. It was time to come out of my room now, since I'd read the story.

As soon as I opened my bedroom door, my mom said, "You'd better be done reading that book, or you are coming out for a restroom break."

To which I replied, "I am done reading the story."

After I explained the story to my mom, she said, "The main reason I wanted you to read that book was for you to know that everything you are afraid of is just your imagination. Ninety-nine percent of the things that you are afraid of are not real, and the other one percent does not harm you. You remind me of Mateo from the story. Never be afraid of ghosts or monsters, because they are not real."

From that day on, I wasn't too afraid anymore. But when it came to the boomerang ghost, that fear was different.

Good Riddance

I thought I have gotten rid of all the fears. Then, on Halloween Day, it all came back. Halloween was on a Saturday that year, so I didn't have school. I went grocery shopping with my mom while dressed up in my princess costume.

As we approached the automatic sliding doors, I said, "Stop for a second, Mom."

"Why?" she asked.

"Look, I can work magic," I replied. Then I waved my wand as I got closer to the doors, and they opened.

"Wow! That was incredible, Sami," she said.

She knew I was just joking because we have been to that grocery store many times, and the doors usually open regardless. When we entered the store, it seemed like a Halloween costume party. Everybody was dressed up, both employees and shoppers, and the store was filled with Halloween decorations. While shopping, my mom let me pick out five of my favorite snacks. I was happy, even though I knew I would need her permission to eat them if I wanted to. But, still, that was nice of her. So I was walking beside a cart full of groceries. It was almost as tall as I was.

When we were done shopping, we went to the register to pay for the items in the cart. When I looked up, there he was: the boomerang ghost.

I shouted, "No! Get me out of here!"

"It's okay, Sami," said my mom. "It's just a store clerk wearing Cheveyo's costume." Then she turned to the clerk and said, "Can you please take off your mask for one second? My daughter is filled with apprehension toward that character ever since she saw the movie."

He said, "Sure," and he willingly took off his mask.

"See?" my mom said.

I saw that it wasn't really Cheveyo, so I was calm. But deep down, that fear was still embedded.

My fear of the ghost was back after seeing the store clerk that day. Now I was back to asking my mom if I could sleep beside her again every night. My insomnia was back again. Not being able to sleep well was very unpleasant, and it had to stop because I could not concentrate on my lessons anymore. I was always falling asleep in class.

One evening, my mom and I were watching TV in the living room, and the show was interesting, but due to my inability to sleep well the past few nights, I fell asleep on the couch by my mom. My mom, the nicest woman on earth, carried me to my room and lay me down on my bed. About seven hours later, I woke up and rolled around in my bed, hoping to find her sleeping by my side. She wasn't there.

Then I realized that I was in my room all alone again. Oh no! There was no way I could sleep there. So I woke up and turned all the lights on. It seemed like the first night all over again. But this time, my fear turned into anger. I was angry at my mom for taking me to my room instead of hers. The only thing different was the thought that my mom might be part of the conspiracy theory—the one that enables Cheveyo to kidnap her daughter easily. I looked out into the hall again, and it was pitch-black. Unlike the first night, this night I didn't have a flashlight.

I anticipated everything that could happen to me if I went out into that hall. For instance, I could bump my head against a wall and get a concussion. Then, while I was on the floor, he could easily get me. Another instance could be Cheveyo pulling me from the hall and into a room— possibly the room my great-grandma died in when I was five years old. That room scared me sometimes.

I decided not to take the risk that night, so I shouted, "Mom!" I could hear my voice as it echoed through the hall. I yelled many times. It seemed like she wasn't going to wake up. Then I thought, "I hope the ghost didn't get my mom, and now he's coming for me!" So I shouted even louder.

Then, a few seconds later, I heard her door open slowly. The lights came on in the hall. "Sami, is that you?" my mom asked. "What's going on?"

"Mommy, I'm scared. Why did you bring me in my room instead of yours?"

"I'm sorry, sweetheart. We really have to do something about this, Samantha."

Then I followed her to her room.

Every day I asked myself, "How do I conquer this fear that has resurfaced?" I couldn't keep asking to sleep beside my mom every night for the rest of my life. Soon, my dad would be back from his deployment. Then he was going to kick me out of their room. I would be sleeping in my room again, all alone.

I loved my dad so much, and I missed him, but I was also glad he hadn't been home for the past few weeks. My dad always said, "You are a tough girl. Tough it out." Those were his exact words. For instance, if I fell and got a scrape on my knees, he would say, "Oh, my poor baby got a boo-boo." Then he would dress my wound, kiss it, and hug me, of course. Then he would say, "Be strong, because you are a tough girl. Tough it out." He would also say, "Show me what you got. Let me see your tough-girl face and muscles."

I usually made a face like an angry and powerful person but with tiny biceps, and I would grunt like I was strong.

Then he'd usually say, "Yeah, give me a high five." And he would walk away.

I would stop crying and would feel like I had overcome the pain.

So if my dad had been there, he would have let me sleep in their room for probably the first night only. And if I said I was scared on the second night, he would decline my stay. He would probably say, "Remember, you are a tough girl, Sami. Now, tough it out. Go back in there, and try to fall asleep." We would do the whole powerful-person-face thing and fist-clenching again. Then I would show him that I could conquer the world. But I could guarantee that when I walked away and shut my bedroom door, the pretentious giant in me would disappear, and I would start sobbing. Why? Because I knew there was something else that was greater than a boo-boo: Mr. Cheveyo.

I never understood how something that is made of wind could overcome a living being. And how did he even throw the boomerang that chops off limbs? Don't you need to have physical hands to do that? And how did he even manage to attack that boy who was asleep?

My dreams are always awesome. Sometimes when I'm dreaming that some bad guys are chasing after me, when I get to the edge of a cliff or a very tall building, I can just spread my arms and fly. Other times, I can just pick up a piece of straw, and it will turn into a magic wand, and then I just destroy them all in an instant. I am pretty sure this can happen in anyone's dream. So how come Cheveyo could attack anyone even while they were sleeping? I would never know. But I had to figure out a way to get rid of my fear of that guy. I thought about this every day. Somehow, somewhere, the gods of thoughts heard mine and relayed them to my mom, or maybe she was just very good at reading minds.

One day, she came home with a movie. "Hey, Sami, I have a video for you to watch," she said.

I was a little surprised because it was a school night. She never lets me watch television on weeknights. But I wasn't complaining about it. I was excited to have a movie date with my mom. I grabbed a snack from the food pantry, and I sat comfortably beside her.

The movie started, and the next thing I saw was a group of awesome Indian people, the Hopi tribe. Then the next scene was just a still picture of a city called Moenkopi. But I remembered seeing that in another movie. And the music in the background sounded like music from a horror movie. All of a sudden, a scene from *The Boomerang Ghost* came on.

I was about to cover my face, but my mom said, "No, I want you to watch it."

"I don't want to watch that scary movie again," I said to her.

"This is not the actual movie you saw," she said. "It is the making of the movie. I want you to learn that the ghost of Cheveyo will never attack you in your dreams because he is not real."

While watching the making of the movie, I realized that Cheveyo was just a character played by a nice kid, and his scary face was all makeup. They showed his ghostly preparation. There were about four people dressing him up with a latex mask and a lot of gooey things to hold them in place. It took a long time to do this. The whole makeup process took about three hours.

During his interview, he stated that almost all the scenes were computer-generated. Sometimes he would stand in front of a green screen and swing his hand like he was throwing a boomerang, but really his hand was empty, and the computer generated the boomerang and all the chopped-off limbs. But for the scene where he was practicing with his boomerang in the field, it really was a boomerang.

The most important part was that, when he was answering questions, he was smiling the whole time. Then I said to myself, "Wait a minute. This boy isn't scary at all. He is just like me, standing in front of a green screen, and the system makes him scary-looking. And the kids that were killed by him were not really dead. They were alive—laughing and having fun. The making of their scenes shows them pretending to be in pain and faking death. Then I thought, "I can watch this movie over and over again in a dark room, alone, and I will never be afraid again after."

The Surprise

"So guys," Samantha said as she finished the story, "I stood up on stage before you all today because of many reasons. The first reason is for you not to be afraid of anything anymore. Like my mom said, ninety-nine percent of the things we are afraid of are all just our imagination, and the other one percent does not harm us. But there *are* some physical things that we still need to be aware of. For instance, if a stranger stops his van and offers you candy, you say *no* and yell for help.

"The second reason is you should always listen and obey your parents and even people who are older than you—for example, your teacher. Your parents always know what's good and bad for you. Whenever they advise you to do something or refrain from doing something, it is for a good reason. If I didn't break my curfew, I never would have watched the scary movie, and I never would have been scared and sleep-deprived for weeks.

"The third reason is to tell you to treat other people the way you want to be treated. If you want to say or do something to somebody, maybe you should think for a second before you continue. Always ask yourself, 'If this was done or said to me, how would I feel?' My main aim today was to show you that you are greater than your fears. But since I'm giving you one life lesson, I thought I should share many more life lessons, considering that I am a few years older than you guys, and I have learned a lot so far, thanks to my mommy. I told you guys a longer version of my story because I wanted it all to make sense at the end, especially the part of the story about me and my friends.

"You will always have your siblings, no matter what. But also, you can have your friends for the rest of your life. Having fun people around you is good. But people only come around if you are a good person, and to be a good person, you need to love and respect other people. Ava, Erica, and I are best friends because of the way we treat each other. If something bad is said to one person and that person is hurt, whoever said it always apologizes. And the other person forgives. My two friends became friends again because of forgiveness. It is always good to forgive—even at home with your siblings. Learn to love each other, and you guys will be happy all the time. And when you are happy all the time, you can grow up as a healthy person.

"Once, I asked my great-granny, who was ninety-eight years old, why she was still having many, many birthdays and why she was so happy every day. She told me that she had a great companion who lived next door to her at the senior home. It was her friend Lucinda. They met in first grade, and they were still friends. They were both ninety-eight years old, and they still played together.

"Then I said, 'I want to still have my friends when I am old as you, Great-Gran,' and she told me what I just told you guys about being a good person.

"Another point I wanted to make is about helping people in need. I told you the story of how we helped Dave the homeless guy because I want you to go out and start doing the same, if you haven't already. If you have two or more of something, and you notice that someone really needs it, you should give them one. Even if you only have one thing, but you don't really need it, give it to that person, and you will have abundance later. It might not be the same day, but you will realize that you have gained even more than what you had before. And if you don't have what the other person needs, don't ever go out and steal from somebody, because stealing is never good. You are probably thinking that you would be doing the right thing by helping the other person, but it turns out that you would be considered a bad person. As you can see in my story, we didn't have anything to help Dave with, but we didn't steal those things. Instead, we figured out a good way to make money to help him.

"Thank you, guys, very much, for listening. And remember, when you get home tonight, if you think there might be a monster in your closet or under your bed, I want you to say, 'I am stronger than you, you nonscary creature!' And you should go take a look in your closet or under the bed. You will see that it is gone—gone forever."

The crowd applauded as Samantha walked off the stage.

Backstage, Samantha got a hug from her mom. "That was incredible, Samantha. Good job!" said her mom.

"Yes, that was amazing, Samantha," said Mrs. Jones. Guess what?"

"What?" asked Samantha.

"Courtesy of the school, you get a gift for your bravery and courage for standing onstage and telling your story," replied Mrs. Jones.

"Thank you," replied Samantha.

"I didn't know your fear was so bad, Sami," said her mom. "Oh, poor kid. Next time, don't hide anything from me, okay? You need to talk to me about everything."

"Okay, Mommy," Samantha replied.

"I love you, kiddo."

"I love you too, Mommy."

◆　◆　◆

A few hours later, Samantha and her mom arrived home.

"Mom, I think someone is in my bedroom," Samantha said.

"How do you know?" asked her mom.

"I remember shutting my bedroom door before we left."

"Come on now, Sami. You just advised a hall full of people not to be afraid of anything, so why are you doing otherwise?" asked her mom.

"Well, I told them not to be afraid of ghosts, monsters, and the dark. It's fine to be aware of kidnappers and burglars, like in this scenario. We might have a burglar in our house, Mom."

"The doors and windows are still intact, and there is no sign of forced entry, so stop being paranoid, Samantha," her mom said.

When Samantha got to her room, she saw someone sitting on her bed. It was her dad!

"Surprise!" he shouted.

"Daddy!" Samantha screamed as she ran toward him and gave him a big hug.

Soon, her mom came running in too, and she also gave him a hug.

"See, I told you there was someone in my room," Samantha said.

"Yes, you were right," said her mom.

"By the way, I could hear you guys talking in the hall about a burglar. If I were a burglar, I could have attacked you two," said her dad.

"Hey, Dad, we were planning to surprise you, but you surprised us instead," said Samantha.

"How were you guys planning to surprise me?" he asked.

"Shh, don't tell him yet, because we can still do it," her mom said.

"Oh, yeah! Let's do it," said Samantha. "Dad, can you step out of the house for a minute, please? You can just stand on the other side of the front door until we tell you to come in, okay?"

"Okay," he replied.

Samantha and her mom quickly gathered the instruments. Samantha placed the keyboard just ten feet away from the front door.

"Are you ready?" asked her mom.

Samantha nodded in reply. She began playing the notes to "You're the Inspiration."

A few seconds before the vocal part, her mom said, "Come in now, honey." She started singing as soon as he walked in.

He tried to hold back the tears as the song evoked nostalgia. He stood there in awe, watching them.

At the end of the song, Samantha's mom asked, "So, what do you think?"

"Wow," he replied. "You remembered. I love it. That song takes me back almost fifteen years. Good job, guys." He hugged and kissed his wife. Then Samantha came over for a big family hug.

"So, Samantha, I heard you wanted to eat at Solo Para Ti. Is that right?" asked her dad.

"Yes, I wanted to try the 'Jake meal.' It sounds delicious," she replied.

"Well, my menu is long out of date now, so maybe it is going to be the 'Samantha meal' next year. So you'd better start deciding what your meal is going to be," he said.

"What do you mean, Dad?" she asked.

"I am taking you and Mommy to Spain for spring break next year."

"Yay! I am so excited!" Samantha shouted.

"Me too!" said her dad. "The place is a bar and restaurant. The restaurant is open during the day, and the bar is open at night. And the dart game is open during the bar time, so I am going to have to play for you. If I win, I will request that the 'Samantha meal' be on the menu. Then we can go and eat there the next day."

"Wow! That is cool. Thanks, Dad!" she said.

"You are welcome," he replied.

"So what will your meal consist of? Oh, let me guess," said her dad. "It is going to include some chicken nuggets and key lime pie on the side, right?"

She laughed and said, "Those are my favorites, but I will have to think about it, Daddy."

The End

Acknowledgments

I would like to give special thanks to the following people:

My mother, Ethel Richards Ziah
My grand parents, Kaye and Kemah Richards
My second set of parents, Michael Hinneh
and Rachel Dogbe-Hinneh
Ibnyansi Kpakah, my guardian through
parts of the Liberian civil war
My favorite uncle, my sensei, Humphrey
Dogbe
Gayle and Stan Grafsgaard, another set of
amazing parents to me
Tanisha White, for being a sister to me

I also want to thank these people, who read earlier drafts
and inspired me to complete this project:

My wife, Rebekah Joy Dogbe of Moorhead,
Minnesota
My buddy, Oliver M. Sailey of Cleveland,
Ohio
Molly Gunkelman-Askegaard of Fargo,
North Dakota

McKenzie Kaitlyn Galster of Minot, North Dakota

Micaela Kempf of Barnesville, Minnesota

Madelyn Elizabeth Ahrens of West Fargo, North Dakota

Julia Dobbins of Moorhead, Minnesota